Once Upon a Time in JAPAN

Once Upon a Time *in* Japan

Translated by
Roger Pulvers & Juliet Winters Carpenter

Illustrated by
Manami Yamada
Tomonori Taniguchi
Nao Takabatake &
Takumi Nishio

PUBLISHED IN COOPERATION WITH
NHK JAPAN BROADCASTING CORPORATION

TUTTLE Publishing
Tokyo | Rutland, Vermont | Singapore

Published by Tuttle Publishing, an imprint of
Periplus Editions (HK) Ltd.

www.tuttlepublishing.com

Copyright © 2015 by NHK Japan Broadcasting Corporation

ISBN 978-4-8053-1359-6

Distributed by

North America, Latin America & Europe
Tuttle Publishing
364 Innovation Drive
North Clarendon, VT 05759-9436 U.S.A.
Tel: 1 (802) 773-8930
Fax: 1 (802) 773-6993
info@tuttlepublishing.com
www.tuttlepublishing.com

Japan
Tuttle Publishing
Yaekari Building, 3rd Floor
5-4-12 Osaki
Shinagawa-ku
Tokyo 141 0032
Tel: (81) 3 5437-0171
Fax: (81) 3 5437-0755
www.tuttle.co.jp
sales@tuttle.co.jp

Asia Pacific
Berkeley Books Pte. Ltd.
61 Tai Seng Avenue #02-12
Singapore 534167
Tel: (65) 6280-1330
Fax: (65) 6280-6290
inquiries@periplus.com.sg
www.periplus.com

First edition
19 18 17 16   10 9 8 7 6 5 4 3 2   1604RR
Printed in China

Contents

A Second Childhood BY ROGER PULVERS

I have a very personal and nostalgic tie to stories such as the ones you have before you in this book. My wife, who is British-Australian, and I brought up our four children in Japan. They were born in Japan and we sent them to Japanese schools. Thanks to their reading and loving the Japanese folktales they were introduced to in their childhood, my wife and I were able to share the joys of reading them for the first time with them. It was as if we were having a second childhood ourselves, and a very Japanese one at that.

But though I say "Japanese," if you strip away those special elements that are tied to Japan—for instance, the myrtle grass bath in "The Wife Who Never Eats"—there is nothing in these stories that would prevent them from being set in almost any country in the world.

In fact, these are moral tales of truly universal value. Their values transcend geography, era and ethnicity. Their themes appeal to us all. Greedy and selfish people are punished and the rewards for generosity and mercy are large. Cooperation and harmony among people are seen as great virtues.

Japan is today a wealthy country, but for most of history its people lived very modest and frugal lives, depending on each other in order to create sufficient food to sustain themselves. While there is an abundance of water in Japan, rice farming depended upon people sharing and looking after water resources. One traditional expression for selfishness is *gaden insui*, which means "drawing all the water into your own rice paddy." Nothing in the village was seen to be more despicable than this. It is the equivalent of the English expression "feathering your own nest" knowing that the other birds may die.

The animals in these stories have all of the traits, both good and bad, of humans. But animals in Japanese folklore are not considered wicked just because they may cause harm to humans. Snakes in many countries may not be seen in a positive light, but in "The Magical Hood" freeing the snake is taken as an act of mercy. It is the snake's fate to be born a snake, and we should not expect it to act in any other way than a snake must act. We should not despise it, but treat it equally as we do other animals, including humans.

And as for the monkey in "The Monkey and the Crabs," he may be crafty and wily, but that's simply his nature. As someone born in the year of the monkey, I felt somewhat uncomfortable translating this story; but in the end the monkey is contrite, so I heaved a sigh of relief as I finished it.

Though I have emphasized the universal qualities underlying these folk tales, there is one thing very Japanese about them that I learned from what is now nearly 50 years' contact with Japan and its people.

When you share a meal with other people, the last slice of sashimi is often left on the plate in the middle ... or the last grapes or the last pieces of chocolate. People abstain from taking these because they do not wish to be seen as being selfish. Sharing by its nature involves compromise and sacrifice. Maintaining the harmony and good nature of the group is more important than satisfying any individuals. Selflessness is, perhaps, the finest Japanese quality.

This quality pervades these stories, and I think that this is the very thing that the world today is in need of more than anything else. Now is the time when we must not draw all of the resources to ourselves, but make sure that there is enough to go around for all humans and all other creatures on the planet.

Dear readers, you too may experience here the pleasures of first encounter with these wonderful stories. May the children reading them see their beauty and wisdom. And may the adults experience a sublime, if brief, second childhood together with them.

ROGER PULVERS, SYDNEY, AUSTRALIA, JUNE 2015

A Magic Key to Wonder and Reality

BY JULIET WINTERS CARPENTER

Once when I was a little girl of about ten, my birthday came when I was on a trip somewhere with my daddy. To my surprise and delight, he took me to a dime store and said I could pick out my own present—anything I wanted. (I suppose there was a price limit, but then again, dime stores weren't exactly Tiffany's.) I remember unhesitatingly selecting a big book of fairy tales and folklore. What may have happened to that book, and whether it had any Japanese tales in it, I'm not sure. But later on I came to love Japan's *mukashi banashi*—"tales of long ago"—as much as any Western fairy tales, or more.

Why do children love fairy tales and folk tales? Perhaps because of their overwhelming strangeness, and at the same time their reassuring administering of justice. Folk tales are a magic key that opens doors of wonder and reality. While delighting in fantasy and whimsy, readers (or listeners, since the tales are above all meant to be *told*) are exposed to all manner of human behavior, and learn to be critical of characters' choices. Tales are the starting-place of wisdom, and their lessons are universal. These three beloved tales from Japan, known to every child, are sure to delight readers of all ages and backgrounds.

As in other countries, the fox in Japan is a cunning trickster, and in "The Fox and the Otter" he gets his comeuppance and then some. This humorous story may call to mind the classic Brer Rabbit stories, but there the weaker trickster—even more cunning than his oppressors—is the hero, and he uses his wiles to get away. Here the fox is in the spotlight, and it is his own greed that does him in—as perhaps the patient otter knew it would.

"The Gratitude of the Crane" is a haunting story that bridges the worlds of animals and humans. This evocative tale of compassion and gratitude reminds us of how our actions affect others, and ultimately ourselves. Japanese folklore contains many variations on the theme of a rescued bird appearing in human guise to repay its savior—generally as a beautiful young woman who becomes daughter to an old couple or, as here, wife to a poor young man. The stories invariably depict loving self-sacrifice, and they end with an act of betrayal—entry to a forbidden room and forbidden knowledge—that destroys the relationship.

"The Tale of the Bamboo Cutter" is unique in that it is adapted from Japan's oldest prose narrative, going back to the tenth century. Western folk tales are often about royal families, and who gets to marry the princess—not a common theme in Japan. Here we have a princess unlike any other. She is found in the hollow of a bamboo, grows magically into a beautiful young woman, and turns out to be from the moon! Who would have expected a tenth-century tale to feature interstellar travel? When a string of suitors shows up, she gives each one an impossible task—she doesn't *want* to get married. The various ways her suitors try to cheat adds to the fun. Even the emperor comes calling, but she won't have him, either, simply "melting away like a shadow" to avoid a messy situation. This princess seems quite modern—spunky, strong, feminine, and nobody's fool. But in the end she too flies home, leaving everyone with only memories.

I am happy to present these wonderful stories. I know my ten-year-old self would have loved them, and I hope they find many new and eager readers.

The Wife Who Never Eats

Once upon a time there was a man who was as stingy as stingy could be.

"What I really need," he muttered to himself while out tilling his fields, "is a wife who will work for me but never eats."

It wasn't long before a woman appeared at the home of this cheapskate.

"I can work like the devil and I never eat, so please make me your wife," she said. And at that, the man took her as his wife.

Now, she really worked like the devil from dawn to dusk, both in the fields and at home, without taking so much as a mouthful to eat, and the man was most pleased with himself.

But ... then he noticed that the amount of rice in his storehouse had begun to get smaller and smaller ever since the woman had come to live with him.

So, one day, after telling her he was off to work and making to go out, he hid himself in the rafters and waited to see what she would do.

What did he see but his wife, who was never supposed to eat anything at all, cooking up an enormous amount of rice in a cauldron. She made a gigantic pile of rice balls with the cooked rice and then, in a flash, let down her long stringy hair to reveal a huge mouth at the very top of her head!

"Yum yum," she said, stuffing the rice balls down her head. "Eat up, eat up! Down the hatch!"

The man's wife was none other than a witch, and he quaked and shivered and shook.

But he returned home that evening as if he had seen nothing, though he was frightened out of his mind.

"You know," he said to her, "I don't think married life's for me. If you leave I'll give you whatever your heart desires. What do you say?"

"Well then," she said, "get me a big wooden tub."

The man went to the market the very next day and bought a big wooden tub.

But no sooner did he come home with the tub than the witch — now looking like the witch that she was — flung him into it and, heaving it over her shoulders, flew off into the mountains, crying out, "Now I've got a souvenir for my fellow witches!"

Though the man was quaking and shivering and shaking with fear, he managed to stretch out his hands and catch hold of a big branch.

He lifted himself out of the tub and ran back toward the village as fast as his legs would take him.

But the witch caught sight of him and started to run after him. Just as she was about to reach out and grab him, he jumped right into a bed of myrtle grass, which thankfully, because it was the month of May, was growing thick and deep.

The witch pushed aside the rush-like leaves of the myrtle grass in hot pursuit. But the sharp pointy tips of the leaves kept poking her in the eyes. Blood streamed out of her eye sockets and down her cheeks.

"Ouch! That hurts!" she shrieked, before collapsing into a heap in the bed and dying right there on the bed of myrtle grass.

To this day, myrtle grass leaves are floated in the bathtub on May 5th, for it is said that this keeps mishaps and dangers at bay. It is on this day that Boys' Day is celebrated … and the bath itself is called a "Myrtle Grass Bath."

The Mill of the Sea

Once upon a time there were two brothers, both of them very poor. The older brother had a heart of gold, while the little brother was nothing but a mean and ungrateful miser.

The older brother shared whatever food he had with people who were going hungry. But the little brother just hoarded his money and his food. It never crossed his mind to share anything with others.

One summer there was a terrible drought, and all the crops in the village failed. The people there were at wits' end as to what to do. The older brother gave what food he had to other people. In the end, he didn't even have a morsel left for himself. So he went to his little brother to borrow some rice.

"It's your fault for giving your rice to those people," said his little brother. "I've got no rice for you."

The older brother plodded back home. He was at the end of his tether. Just then, an old man with a long white beard appeared before him.

"For so long you've been very kind to others," he said, handing him a small stone mill. "This is for you. Turn the handle to the right and the mill will give you whatever you wish for. To stop it, turn the handle back to the left."

Having said that, the old man vanished into thin air.

The older brother started turning the mill to the right the minute he got home, saying, "I wish for rice ... I wish for rice."

Lo and behold, if rice didn't come spilling out of the mill!

From then on the mill provided everything his heart desired. It built him a grand house where he held lavish banquets, inviting the villagers to come and eat their fill. And when the meals were over, he had the mill make sweets for his guests to take home to their families.

The little brother, though, was convinced that his older brother was hiding something from him. So he sneakily followed him and saw him turning the wheel to bring all sorts of things into the world. And when his older brother had fallen fast asleep, he snatched the mill and the leftover sweets and shot out of the house.

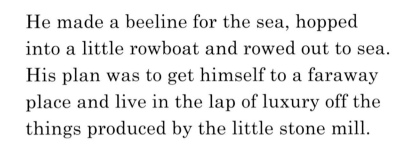

He made a beeline for the sea, hopped
into a little rowboat and rowed out to sea.
His plan was to get himself to a faraway
place and live in the lap of luxury off the
things produced by the little stone mill.

After a while, though, all the rowing had
made him very hungry, so he gobbled
down the sweets he had taken from his
brother's home. This made him crave
something salty.

"I wish for salt ... I wish for salt," he said,
turning the mill's handle to the right.

Salt started to stream out of the mill, and he was over the moon with joy. But the mill just continued to spew out salt until the little rowboat was absolutely overflowing with it.

"Stop … stop!" he screamed in a panic. But the mill didn't stop pouring salt into the rowboat, despite his pleas.

In the end, the little rowboat sank, taking the little brother with it right down to the bottom of the sea.

It is said that the stone mill sits to this day on the seabed, turning round and round, ceaselessly pouring out salt. And that, apparently, is what makes the sea as salty as it is.

The Monkey and the Crabs

A monkey was trudging along a mountain path one day, talking to himself.

"Oh, I'm so hungry I could eat a horse," he muttered. "Isn't there anywhere I can find something to eat?"

Just then he came upon a persimmon seed on the ground.

"Can't exactly fill my belly up with this," he complained.

A mother crab happened by carrying a rice ball in her pincers, and the monkey, scheming to pinch it from her, said, "Why, good day, Mrs. Crab! I've got something really splendid here for you. It's a persimmon seed. See? All you've got to do is plant it, and you'll have more persimmons than you can shake a stick at."

"But there are hungry children waiting for me at home, and I have to get back with this rice ball for them."

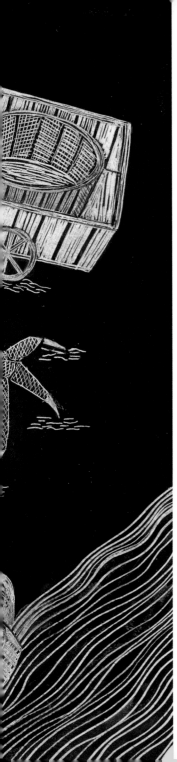

"But look, eat a rice ball and what's left of it?
Nothing. A persimmon seed, on the other hand,
will give you fruit every year."

The crab was in two minds, but eventually she
traded the rice ball for the seed.

She planted the seed the moment she got home,
then she and her children watered the plant,
waving their pincers about and singing this song ...

"If you don't hurry and sprout
We'll snip you right out!
Hurry and sprout, hurry and sprout
Hurry little seed ... hurry and sprout!"

Believe it or not, a little sprout sprouted right out of
the ground and started to grow leaves.

Before they knew it, the sprout was a tree and the tree was bearing fruit over all its branches. The mother crab and her children were jumping for joy. But, try as she may, she just couldn't climb up the trunk of the tree. Just when they were wondering what they could do, the monkey came by.

"Leave the picking to me," he said.

The monkey dashed up the tree, and the crabs watched helplessly as he picked the sweet ripe red persimmons and made a pig out of himself, eating all of them, tossing the hard bitter green ones down to them.

Some of the hard fruit landed on the mother crab's head, injuring her. So the children crabs scampered off in a huff to fetch help from their friends — the mortar, the bee and the chestnut.

The mortar, the bee and the chestnut came back in no time, deciding that they would give the monkey his due in his own home.

When they got there, the monkey was out. So the mortar rolled up to the roof, the bee hid under the lid of a big water pot and the chestnut half-buried itself in the ashes of the open hearth.

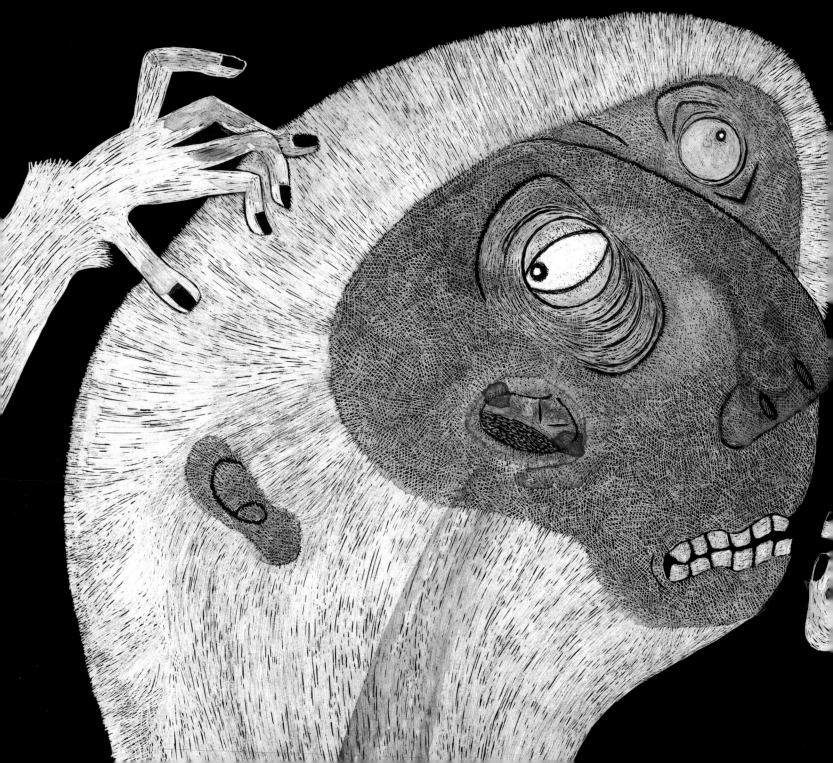

The monkey came home and went right to the open hearth.

"Brrr, it's freezing!" he said, rubbing his hands over the hot ashes ... when suddenly, the chestnut burst open with a loud bang and sailed smack into the monkey's face.

"Ow, that burns! Ow ow ow!" he shrieked, scurrying over to the water pot and lifting its lid ... when suddenly, the bee flew out and stung him right in the face.

"Ow, that stings! Ow ow ow!" he shrieked, rushing outside ...

... when suddenly, the mortar came
tumbling down, aiming straight for
his head.

"I'm sorry. I'll never be bad again,"
said the monkey, bowing in front of
all of them on his hands and knees.

After that, the monkey and the
crabs lived in peace with each
other forever and a day.

The Magical Hood

Once upon a time there lived a young man who was a very hard worker. He was on his way home as usual one night after a long day's work when he happened upon some children who were being cruel to a fox cub they had caught by the side of the road.

"Hey!" shouted the young man, chasing the children away. "Stop torturing an innocent animal like that!"

Then he turned to the cub.

"Now, take care you don't get caught again," he smiled.

The cub seemed to smile too as she headed for the hills.

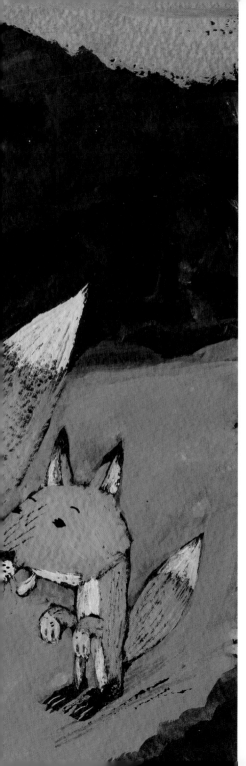

The young man was on his way home from the fields the next day when the very same fox cub and her mother appeared as if out of nowhere by the side of the road.

"Thank you very much for saving my child. Please accept this hood as a token of my gratitude," she said, handing him a well-worn little hood.

"This is no ordinary hood. If you put this hood on your head you will be able to understand what animals are saying to each other."

Before he knew it, the fox and her cub were gone.

The young man wasn't sure if he believed his ears, so he immediately put the hood on his head. No sooner had he done this than he heard the voices of young women.

"There's plenty of rice for the taking in that paddy over there."

"Oh, really? Then I'm going to be there first thing in the morning to eat some."

"Yeah, but just make sure you don't get shooed away by that scary old lady!"

The young man looked up and saw two little birds chirping away to each other. It was that chirping that he had overheard!

"Hmm, this is fascinating," he thought. "I'm going to listen in as much as I can."

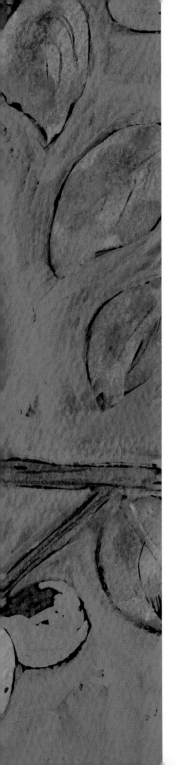

Two crows were cawing to each other in the branches. The young man put the hood on his head again.

"Hey, long time no see," said one of the crows in a deep husky voice. "So, what's been happening in your village, eh?"

"You've got to hear this," said the other crow. "I mean, the rich merchant's daughter got sick as a dog, and a snake got caught in the roof when they were re-thatching it."

"You don't say! So the snake must have had something against them for getting caught and took it out on the daughter."

"Yeah, for sure. All they'd have to do is set the snake free and she'd be right as rain. But, you know, human beings have such thick skulls they just don't get it. I feel so sorry for them!"

"This won't do!" thought the young man as he hurried off to the merchant's home, before long standing before its main gate.

"A little bird told me that the merchant's daughter isn't well," he said to the gatekeeper. "Give me the chance and I can make her better."

The merchant, who had been at a total loss for what to do for his daughter, immediately invited the young man into his home.

"There's a snake caught in the roof that you're re-thatching," the young man told the merchant, "and he's in a lot of pain. If you save the snake, your daughter will get better in two shakes of a lamb's tail."

The rich merchant sent one of his servants up into the roof where, sure enough, a snake was caught between it and the ceiling. The servant freed the snake, which had gone all limp.

"There, there, you poor little thing," said the merchant, giving the snake water and letting it go in the garden. "Everything's going to be fine now."

And what do you know! The face of his daughter turned from a pale white to a rosy-cheek red before their very eyes ... and by day's end she was up and about and feeling her old self again. The merchant was beside himself with joy.

"Young man, you've managed to save my daughter and I thank you. She owes you her life. This is a sign that you two were meant for each other. How about it? Would you take my daughter's hand in marriage and look after her forever and ever?"

And that is how the young man and the merchant's daughter became husband and wife ... and lived happily ever after.

Sleepyhead Taro and the Children

O nce upon a time a very poor mother and son lived happily together, farming the land. The son was called Taro. They barely made enough to live on, though they both worked without rest, day in and day out. The land was barely fertile, and they were so plagued by droughts that they ran out of things to eat. Taro's mother fell ill and died from exhaustion, leaving him all alone.

Overcome by sadness, Taro wept and wept and went on weeping until long after her funeral … and then he fell into a very deep sleep.

He slept and slept and slept some more. The neighbors were sick with worry and came to visit him, but he was dead to the world. They cooked food and brought it to him, and he did eat it, but without waking up even for a second.

Village officials arrived and hollered in Taro's ears, but he remained sound asleep. The children from around there came and tickled his feet. His feet jiggled about, but he himself didn't so much as blink an eye.

Before anyone knew it three years had passed, and the fields and paddies by Taro's house were blanketed in weeds.

Then, one morning, Taro suddenly woke up. He went straight out into the fields and paddies, got rid of the weeds that had grown as tall as he was, and threw himself into tilling the soil. People were shocked to see him.

"Sleepyhead Taro has come out of his three-year sleep!" they cried.

The drought in the village was as bad as it had ever been, and when Taro became aware of this, he headed out to the river with a hoe over his shoulder. A man from the village asked him what he was planning to do at the river. "I'm going to dig a channel for the water," he replied.

"But the river is far away from here," laughed the man. "You're crazy if you think you can dig a channel with a single hoe."

Taro went on his way nonetheless.

"Hey, let's all lend Taro a hand!" said the village children when they heard about what he was going to do. They all lined up behind Taro and followed him to the river.

Taro sunk his hoe deep into the earth by the river. He dug and he dug and he dug some more, and the children dug too, just like him.

The children's parents were anxious about them and went to the river. They were deeply moved to see Taro and the children clutching their hoes and digging a water channel as if their lives depended on it, and they pitched in themselves alongside their children.

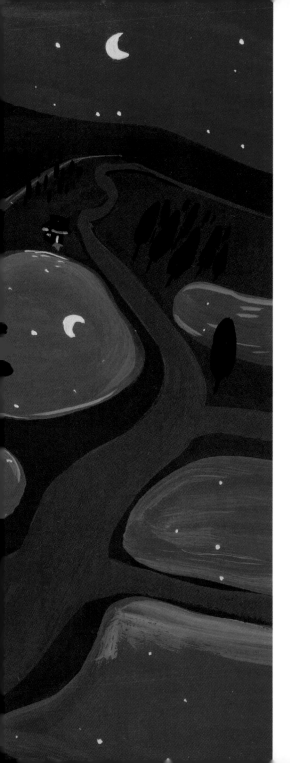

The sun was sitting on the western horizon by the time the channel finally reached the rice paddies in the village. Water from the river came streaming along the channel, bursting into them.

"We did it!" they all cried out to each other. "Thank you, Taro. Thank you so much!"

After that, the village boasted wonderful rice harvests, even when there was a drought. It was all thanks to the water that ran from the river along the channel to their paddies. The village prospered. And Taro continued to work the earth, living in perfect harmony with everyone around him.

The Fox and the Otter

*O*nce upon a time, there was a fox who lived in the mountains and an otter who lived by a river. One day, the fox paid a call on the otter. "Brother Otter," he said, "have you got anything good to eat?"

The otter generously caught a big mess of fish and served it to the fox.

When he had eaten his fill, the fox said, "Mm, that was delicious. Next time I'll treat you to a mountain feast."

The next day, the otter visited the fox. "Well, Brother Fox, I'm here. Bring on the feast!" But the fox just lay staring up at the ceiling without a word. The otter went home in a huff.

The next day, the fox called on the otter again. "Oh, Brother Otter! Sorry about yesterday. The god of the house ordered me to guard the ceiling, so I couldn't chat."

"I see. Well, since you're here, won't you have some fish?" The otter generously treated the fox again. When he was full, the fox said, "Mm, that was delicious! Drop by tomorrow and I promise you a real mountain feast."

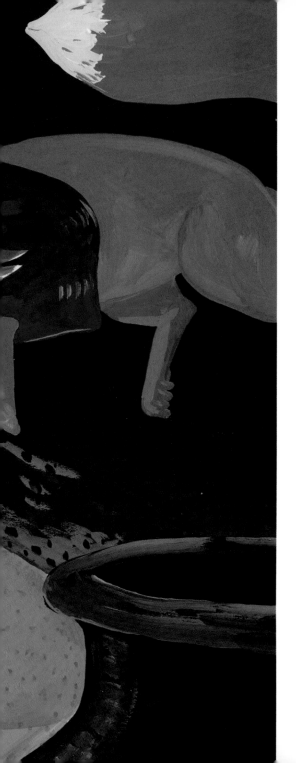

The next day, the otter went back to the fox's den. "Hello, Brother Fox, I'm here for the feast!"

This time the fox just kept looking down at the ground and wouldn't answer. The otter went home furious, thinking he had been tricked again.

The next day, the fox went to see the otter. "Sorry about yesterday, my friend," he said. "The god of the ground ordered me to guard the ground, so I couldn't chat."

Brazenly he went on, "Tell me, Brother Otter, how can I catch a lot of fish, the way you do?"

"Nothing to it," said the otter. "On a freezing cold day, go to the river and dangle your tail in the water. Hold perfectly still, and you'll get a bite in no time."

So one cold day, the fox went to the river and dangled his tail in the chilly water. The sun went down, and soon it was pitch dark. The river water became even colder. Just then the fox felt something brush his tail. "Hurrah! I've caught a fish!"

The fox wanted a big catch, so despite the cold he lingered on, dangling his tail in the freezing river until finally it was so heavy he could hardly move it.

"Oh boy! I hit the jackpot!" The fox tried to jerk his tail up — but it wouldn't budge. He turned around and was shocked to see that the river had turned to solid ice.

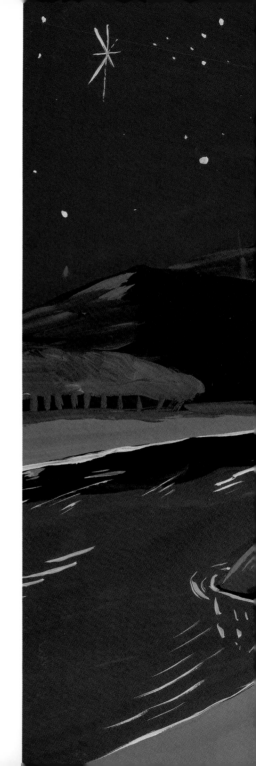

The fox stayed that way till morning, unable to move. Then the villagers discovered him and came storming up. "Look, there's the rascally fox that's always raiding our crops! Catch him! Don't let him get away!"

Frantic to escape, the fox pulled and pulled with all his might.

Then what do you think happened? The tail tore right off, and the fox went running back to the mountains, yelping in pain all the way home.

The Gratitude of the Crane

Once upon a time, there was a kind young man who lived all alone. One winter morning, he went outside and saw a crane caught in a trap, struggling desperately to free itself.

"Wait a moment and I'll set you free," he said.

As soon as the young man undid the rope, the graceful bird rose into the sky, circled overhead three times, and flew off toward the mountains.

One evening a few days later, someone tapped at the young man's door. He opened the door to find a beautiful young woman standing there.

"Sir," she said, "I am a traveler, but it grew dark before I could find an inn. Please, may I stay here for the night?"

The young man let her in, saying, "By all means."

The young woman set right to work and made herself useful. She was sweet-natured besides. In no time, the young man was smitten.

"I'd like you to stay forever," he said. She nodded, and soon they were married

One day, the young man's wife said she wanted to weave some cloth, and asked for thread. After he went and fetched her some, she said, "I will do my weaving at the loom in the shed. You must promise never to look."

The young man promised. She disappeared into the shed, and soon he heard the clackety-clack of the loom.

The next day she went to the shed again and stayed there all day.

After two or three more days, she came out holding pure white cloth — the most beautiful cloth he had ever seen.

"Take this to town and sell it," she said.

In town, the cloth sold for a very high price. The young man was delighted. From then on, every time his wife wove cloth, he would take it to town and sell it. Her cloth became the talk of the town, and its price soared.

The young man wondered how on earth she could weave such beautiful cloth, but since she had forbidden him to look in on her, he resisted the temptation to peek.

However, he could not help noticing that each time she wove a cloth she appeared thinner and more worn.

One day, after she had gone to the shed as usual, the young man's curiosity got the better of him. Very quietly, he slid the door open a crack and peered in.

Imagine how astonished he was when he saw, sitting at the loom, not his bride, but a crane!

The crane was plucking out its feathers and weaving them into cloth. The young man gulped and hurriedly closed the door.

After a while, his wife came out of the shed carrying a bolt of snow-white cloth. Quietly she said, "Now you know. I am the crane whose life you saved. I wanted to stay with you forever, but now that you have seen me in my true form, I can no longer remain. This cloth is the last I will ever weave. Please take it to town and sell it. Thank you for everything. I wish you well."

Then she changed into a crane, flew up into the sky and circled overhead three times before winging her way toward the mountains. The young man stood watching after her, on and on until he could see her no more.

The Tale of the Bamboo Cutter

Once upon a time, there was an old man who cut bamboo to weave baskets.

One day he went into the bamboo forest as usual, and came upon a stalk that was glowing with a mysterious light.

Nestled inside it was a darling, tiny girl. The old man carried her home in his hands, and he and his wife brought her up like their own daughter.

In just three months, the girl grew into a beautiful young woman. Her beauty lit up every corner of the house, so the old couple named her "Princess Kaguya," which means "Shining Night."

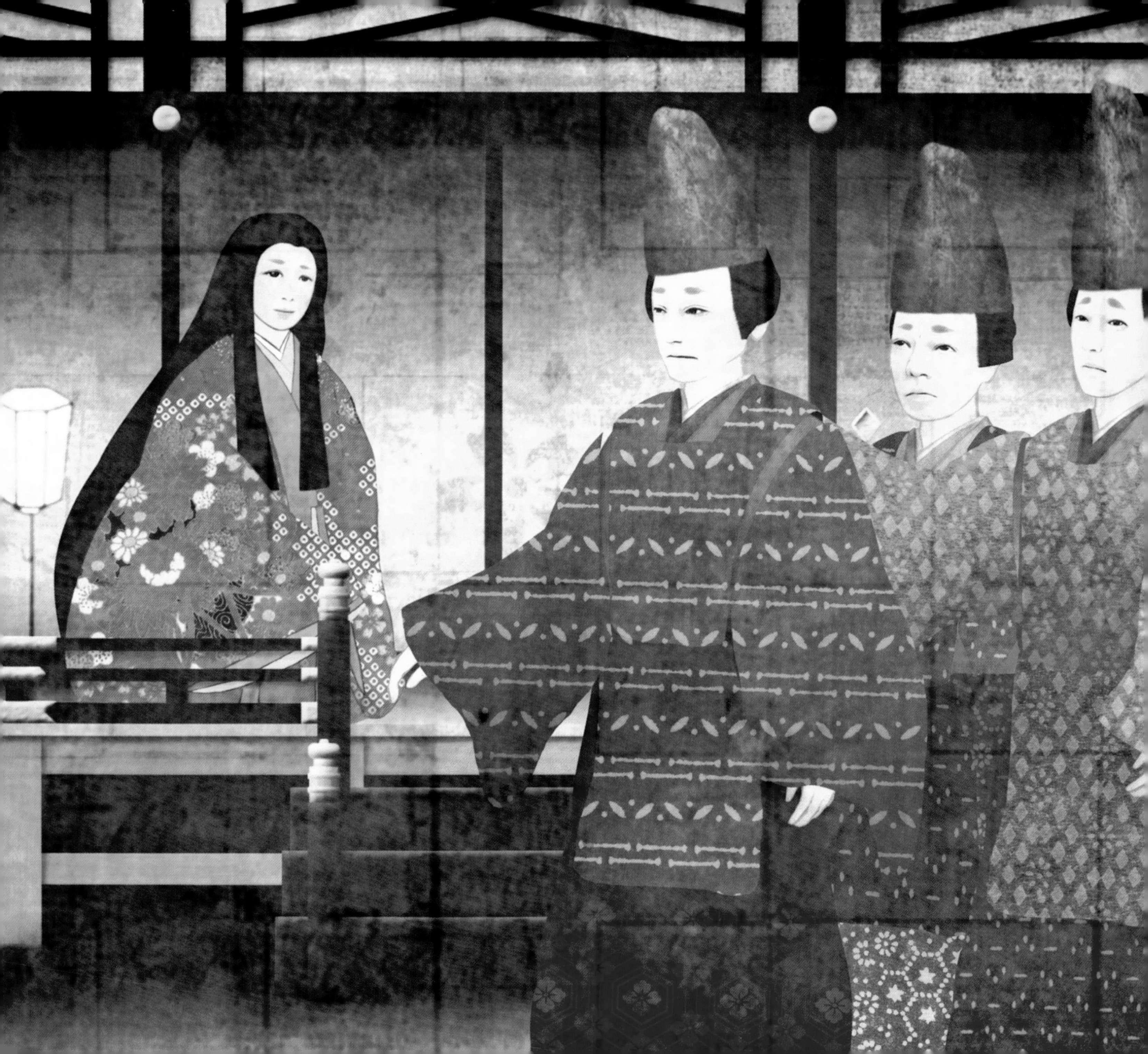

Five noblemen heard of Princess Kaguya's beauty and came forward to ask for her hand in marriage. The old man asked her to choose one of them herself.

She would rather have turned them all down, but in order to please her father, unwillingly she said that she would marry whoever brought her what she asked of him. All of her requests were next to impossible.

One of the suitors, a prince, she told to go
to legendary Mount Horai and bring back
a branch from a tree with a trunk of gold,
branches of silver, and fruit of white jade.

Instead, he had fine craftsmen prepare a
fake. It was so well made that the princess
was stunned. Just as she was thinking she
might have to marry the prince after all,
the head craftsman came along demanding
to be paid, and the trickery was exposed.

Another suitor was told to bring her a
jewel from a dragon's neck, and sent
his men off in search of it. A year went
by with no word from them, so he
decided to set out on his own.

His boat ran into a terrible storm and
he was tossed to and fro in the waves,
barely making it back alive.

A different admirer was given the task of
fetching a cowrie shell laid by a swallow.
While he was removing one from a swallow's
nest in a pillar in the palace kitchen, he lost
his footing and fell. In his hand he held not
the shell, but a piece of swallow poop.

The remaining two suitors also failed.
One was supposed to bring her a
Buddha's begging bowl that glowed,
but his bowl didn't glow at all.

The other was supposed to bring her an
unburnable bag, but his bag burned to a crisp.

Finally the emperor himself heard about the
princess and came calling. Struck by her beauty, he
went up to her, but she melted away like a shadow.
So even the emperor was forced to give up.

Three years went by, and Princess Kaguya took to gazing sadly at the moon. The old man asked her what was wrong.

She said, "I am from the moon. On the fifteenth of August, when they come for me, I will have to go back." This made the old man very sad, and he asked the emperor to protect her.

Soon it was the fifteenth, the night of the full moon. Two thousand imperial soldiers stood guard around the house.

All at once the sky lit up. A band of people came riding down on clouds and lined up above the ground. The soldiers were overcome by a strange force, and only looked on in a daze.

Princess Kaguya was hiding
in the storehouse, held tightly
in the old woman's arms, but
when the leader of the moon
people demanded her return,
the door mysteriously opened,
and she slipped out.

The old couple collapsed in helpless tears. The princess left them her kimono as a memento, and in its place she was given a wrap worn by heavenly beings. The moment she put it on, all her sadness and concern for the people of Earth were gone.

She was led into a flying chariot,
and vanished into the heavens.

NHK World

NHK World is the international service of Japanese public broadcaster NHK. The stories published in this book were part of a special series produced by Radio Japan, NHK World's radio service in 18 languages.

TRANSLATORS

Roger Pulvers is an author, playwright, theatre director, translator and journalist. He has published more than 40 books in Japanese and English, most recently a novel written in Japanese, *Hoshizuna Monogatari*, and his memoirs, *If There Were No Japan*. Roger was assistant to director Nagisa Oshima on the film *Merry Christmas, Mr. Lawrence*. He has received several awards, including the Crystal Simorgh Prize for Best Script at the 27th Fajr International Film Festival in Tehran, the Miyazawa Kenji Prize and the Noma Award for the Translation of Japanese Literature.

Juliet Winters Carpenter is an American translator of modern Japanese literature. She studied Japanese literature at the University of Michigan and is a professor of English at Doshisha Women's College of Liberal Arts in Kyoto. She is a double recipient of the Japan-U.S. Friendship Commission Prize for the Translation of Japanese Literature, once in 1980 for *Secret Rendezvous*, her translation of Kobo Abe's *Mikkai*, and again in 2014-2015 for *A True Novel*, her translation of Minae Mizumura's *Honkaku Shosetsu*.

ILLUSTRATORS

After working as a graphic designer, Manami Yamada became an author of children's books and an artist. Her books include *Grandma Nosehair*, whose Illustrations were selected for the Bologna Illustrators Exhibition in 2008, and *Kaeru to Okan* ("The Frog and the Crown"). She is the recipient of several awards.

Tomonori Taniguchi was born in Osaka in 1978, and studied *Nihon-ga* Japanese painting at Kanazawa College of Art. His children's books have been published in Japan, France and Italy. They include *Sarukun to Banana no Yuenchi* ("Monkey and Banana's Amusement Park") and *Pinocchio, la marionnette de fer* ("Pinocchio the Iron Puppet").

Born in Gifu prefecture in 1978, Nao Takabatake is an author of children's books and an illustrator. He received the Japan Picture Book Award in 2013 for *Kaeru no Odekake* ("The Frog Goes Out"). His other works include *Chiita Dai Se-ru* ("Cheetah's Big Sale") and *Banana Jiken* ("The Banana Incident").

Takumi Nishio was born in Tokyo in 1968. He worked as graphic and set designer for public broadcaster NHK from 1994 to 1999, and later produced animation, illustrations and opening titles for TV programs. He currently teaches at the Yokohama College of Art and Design.

NARRATOR

Yuko Aotani was born in Yokohama and spent five years in London until the age of 14. After graduating from Sophia University in Tokyo, she joined NHK as a bilingual reporter and went on to anchor several news programs on NHK World. Now a freelancer, she is active in a variety of fields ranging from news, culture, and education to voice work.